Silly Milly
and the Picture Day Sillies

Silly Milly
y las tonterías del día de la foto

Written by
Laurie Friedman

Illustrated by
Lauren Rodriguez

Translation by
Milly Blanco

Escrito por
Laurie Friedman

Ilustrado por
Lauren Rodriguez

Traducción de
Milly Blanco

A Blossoms Beginning Readers Book
Un libro de Los Lectores Florecientes

Crabtree Publishing
crabtreebooks.com

BLOSSOMS BEGINNING READERS LEVEL GUIDE

Level 1 Early Emergent Readers Grades PK-K
Books at this level have strong picture support with carefully controlled text and repetitive patterns. They feature a limited number of words on each page and large, easy-to-read print.

Level 2 Emergent Readers Grade 1
Books at this level have a more complex sentence structure and more lines of text per page. They depend less on repetitive patterns and pictures. Familiar topics are explored, but with greater depth.

Level 3 Early Readers Grade 2
Books at this level are carefully developed to tell a great story, but in a format that children are able to read and enjoy by themselves. They feature familiar vocabulary and appealing illustrations.

Level 4 Fluent Readers Grade 3
Books at this level have more text and use challenging vocabulary. They explore less familiar topics and continue to help refine and strengthen reading skills to get ready for chapter books.

School-to-Home Support for Caregivers and Teachers

This book helps children grow by letting them practice reading. Here are a few guiding questions to help the reader with building his or her comprehension skills. Possible answers appear here in red.

Before Reading:
- What do I think this story will be about?
  - *I think this story will be about a girl named Milly who likes to act silly.*
  - *I think this story will be about picture day.*

During Reading:
- Pause and look at the words and pictures. Why did the character do that?
  - *I think Milly is being silly on picture day because she likes to make Jack laugh.*
  - *I think Milly's mom does not like her being silly today because she wants the picture to look nice.*

After Reading:
- Describe your favorite part of the story.
  - *My favorite part was when Milly and Jack were having fun being silly together.*
  - *I liked the part when Milly and her family were silly together.*

Milly likes to be silly.
A Milly le gusta ser tonta.

Milly likes to be silly with Jack.
Jack is a baby.
Jack is Milly's baby brother.

A Milly le gusta hacerse la tonta con Jack.
Jack es un bebé.
Jack es el hermano menor de Milly.

Today is picture day.
Mom is taking Milly and Jack to have their picture taken.

Hoy es el día de las fotos.
Mamá se lleva a Milly y a Jack para que les tomen una foto.

Milly smiles very silly.
Milly says, "Cheese."
Jack claps. Jack laughs.

Milly sonríe muy tontamente.
Milly dice: "Queso."
Jack aplaude. Jack se ríe.

"Cheese," says Milly. "Cheese. Cheese. Cheese."

"Queso," dice Milly. "Queso. Queso. Queso."

"Today is picture day," says Mom.

"Hoy es el día de las fotos," dice mamá.

"Today is NOT a good day to be silly," says Mom.

"Hoy NO es un buen día para ser tonta," dice mamá.

But Milly likes to be silly.
Jack likes when Milly is silly.

Pero a Milly le gusta ser tonta.
A Jack le gusta cuando Milly es tonta.

"Are you ready?" asks Mom.
Milly is ready.

"¿Estás lista?" pregunta mamá.
Milly está lista.

Milly is ready to have her picture taken.
Milly meets the man who will take her picture.
His name is Ted.

Milly está lista para que le tomen la foto.
Milly conoce al hombre que va a tomarle la foto.
Su nombre es Ted.

Ted tells Milly to sit in a chair.
Jack sits next to Milly.

Ted le dice a Milly que se siente en la silla.
Jack se sienta junto a Milly.

Ted counts to three.
"Say cheese," says Ted.

Ted cuenta hasta tres.
"Di queso," dice Ted.

Milly smiles very silly.
Milly says, "Cheese."
Jack laughs. Jack claps.

Milly sonríe muy tontamente.
Milly dice: "Queso."
Jack se ríe. Jack aplaude.

"Cheese," says Milly.
"Cheese. Cheese. Cheese."
Jack likes when Milly is silly.

"Queso," dice Milly.
"Queso. Queso. Queso."
A Jack le gusta cuando Milly es tonta.

But Mom does not like it.
Not today.
"Today is NOT a good day to be silly," says Mom.

Pero a mamá no le gusta.
Hoy no.
"Hoy NO es un buen día para ser tonta," dice mamá.

Milly and Jack sit in the chair.
Ted counts to three.
"Say cheese," says Ted.

Milly y Jack se sientan en la silla.
Ted cuenta hasta tres.
"Di queso," dice Ted.

Milly does not even say cheese.
But Jack claps. Jack laughs.
Milly claps. Milly laughs too.

Milly ni siquiera dice queso.
Pero Jack aplaude. Jack se ríe.
Milly aplaude. Milly también se ríe.

Milly and Jack have the sillies.
Milly is happy. Jack is happy.

Milly y Jack están haciendo tonterías.
Milly está feliz. Jack está feliz.

Mom is not happy.
Ted is not happy.

Mamá no está feliz.
Ted no está contento.

Mom tells Milly and Jack to sit in the chair.
"NO more sillies!" says Mom.

Mamá les dice a Milly y Jack que se sienten en la silla.
"¡NO más tonterías!" dice mamá.

"Today is picture day," says Mom.
"Today is NOT a good day to be silly."

"Hoy es el día de la foto," dice mamá.
"Hoy NO es un buen día para ser tontos."

Mom looks at Milly.
"Milly," says Mom. "You are the big sister. It is up to you to show Jack what to do."

Mamá mira a Milly.
"Milly," dice mamá. "Usted es la hermana mayor. Depende de ti mostrarle a Jack qué hacer."

"Do you understand?" asks Mom.
Milly understands.

"¿Lo entiendes?" pregunta mamá.
Milly lo entiende.

Milly sits in the chair.
Jack sits in the chair
"No more sillies," Milly tells Jack.

Milly se sienta en la silla.
Jack se sienta en la silla.
"No más tonterías," le dice Milly a Jack.

Ted counts to three.
"Smile," says Ted.
Milly smiles. Jack smiles.
Ted takes the picture.

Ted cuenta hasta tres.
"Sonríe," dice Ted.
Milly sonríe. Jack sonríe.
Ted toma la foto.

Ted shows the picture to Mom.
Mom smiles. Ted smiles.
Ted le muestra la foto a mamá.
Mamá sonríe. Ted sonríe.

Mom is proud of Milly.
Mom is proud of Jack.

Mamá está orgullosa de Milly.
Mamá está orgullosa de Jack.

But sometimes it is.
Sometimes it is a very good time to be silly.

Pero a veces lo es.
A veces es muy bueno el momento para hacer tonterías.

ABOUT THE AUTHOR

Laurie Friedman is the award-winning author of more than seventy-five critically acclaimed picture books, chapter books, and novels for young readers, including the bestselling *Mallory McDonald* series and the *Love, Ruby Valentine* series. She is a native Arkansan, and in addition to writing, loves to read, bake, do yoga, and spend time with her friends and family. For more information about Laurie and her books, please visit her website at www.lauriebfriedman.com.

ABOUT THE ILLUSTRATOR

Lauren Rodriguez is an illustrator and character designer in the LA area. She loves passion fruit tea, nighttime, paranormal podcasts, and her two doggies (Annie and Teddy).

Written by: Laurie Friedman
Illustrations by: Lauren Rodriguez
Art direction and layout by: Rhea Wallace
Series Development: James Earley
Proofreader: Kathy Middleton
Educational Consultant: Marie Lemke M.Ed.
Print and production coordinator: Katherine Berti

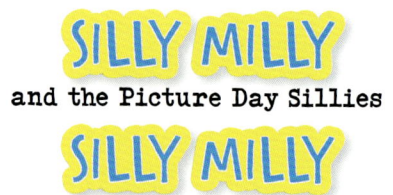

SILLY MILLY and the Picture Day Sillies

SILLY MILLY y las tonterías del día de la foto

Crabtree Publishing

crabtreebooks.com   800-387-7650
Copyright © 2023 Crabtree Publishing
All rights reserved. No part of this publication may be reproduced, stored in a retrieval system or be transmitted in any form or by any means, electronic, mechanical, photocopying, recording, or otherwise, without the prior written permission of Crabtree Publishing Company.

Printed in China/082022/FE052422CT

Published in Canada
Crabtree Publishing
616 Welland Ave.
St. Catharines, Ontario
L2M 5V6

Published in the United States
Crabtree Publishing
347 Fifth Avenue,
Suite 1402-145
New York, NY, 10016

Library and Archives Canada Cataloguing in Publication
Available at the Library and Archives Canada

Library of Congress Cataloging-in-Publication Data
Available at the Library of Congress

Paperback: 9781039624658
Ebook: 9781039625495
Epub: 9781039625075